Dogs of Myth

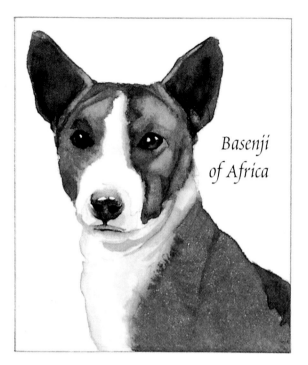

Basenji
of Africa

Rottweiler
of Europe

Coyote of the
Americas

Akita
of Asia

Dogs of Myth

TALES FROM AROUND THE WORLD

Gerald and Loretta Hausman

Illustrated by Barry Moser

SCHOLASTIC INC.

NEW YORK TORONTO LONDON AUCKLAND SYDNEY
MEXICO CITY NEW DELHI HONG KONG

For Zeb, Beeper, and Mocha
—G. H. AND L. H.

To the memory of the father I never knew—
Arthur Boyd Moser, 1911–1941
—B. M.

ISBN 0-439-27611-X

12 11 10 9 8 7 6 5 4 3 2 1   1 2 3 4 5 6/0

Printed in the U.S.A.   14

First Scholastic printing, January 2001

Cover design by Anahid Hamparian

Contents

"FRIEND IS A DOG'S NAME."

—*Jamaican Proverb*

Dogs of Myth

Introduction

DOGS HAVE BEEN with us since the first stargazer cast an eye to the heavens. Were dogs up there, too—in the stars? The answer is yes. The Dog Star guided and guarded, just as its counterpart, Dog, did here on earth. Inseparable from people, in caves and in castles, dogs have watched, warned, sported, lazed, lounged, and loved human beings probably more than any other earthly animal.

And so, the stories in this collection are devoted to the indispensable dog, our most forgiving friend. Here are thirteen myths that reveal the deep bond that began some six thousand years ago in Africa. Well, some say much before that—with the Afghan whose wet nose plugged the holes in Noah's Ark, but that is another story.

Our canine heroes include the dog who first brought fire to humankind, the dog who taught us to laugh, and the great one who sacrificed himself for his friend. These oral folktales have come from all around the world, and they are not only a reflection of world mythology, but also a portrait of different cultures.

In times gone by, dogs were princes, kings, ninjas, necromancers, politicians, shape-shifters, gods, and guardians. And in the past, people saw dogs differently from the way we do today. During the Han Dynasty of China, for instance, there was a Shar-pei, who became the first dog to marry a princess. Or, take the patient, all-seeing Saluki, who, according to legend, guarded seven sleeping youths for 309 years. Mythology shows us the same dog that sleeps at our feet and barks at the mail carrier.

However, we also meet the dog of dreams—the superdog who sets the imagination free. There is the princely poodle of London, who could change into anything he wanted. The sturdy Rottweiler of Germany, who carried thunder in his throat. The treasure-giving spaniel, whose paw sprouted diamonds.

Yet these are just a few of the stories that tell about the origins of our canine companions. So, step softly now into that fresh dawn, when a man went out for a walk in the light, and found Dog.

The Creation Dog

THE FIRST MORNING of the world, no one knew what gods ruled the waters, the earth, the mountains, or the heavens. All that people knew was that they were a part of everything and everything was a part of them. But of every individual thing—each lacy leaf and diamond dewdrop—they knew nothing, except wonder. So it was, then, that a man named Nkhango went out for a walk in the light of the world to see what he might see.

And the very first thing that Nkhango saw was something sparkling in a clearing. Before it, paws folded, sat a dog, guarding.

"What strangeness is this?" Nkhango asked.

"You have arrived at my master's dominion," the dog said.

"Who are you?" asked Nkhango.

"I am called Rukuba, Guardian of Fire," the dog answered.

Nkhango saw that the thing Rukuba watched was hungry and that it clamored for more food. Rukuba got up from where he sat and, reaching into an enormous woodpile, fed the fire some of its favorite food, which was wood. The fire was excited to receive the food, and it clapped wildly with its bright, flashing hands.

"What is this thing you have here, Rukuba?" Nkhango asked.

He was charmed by the leaping light, for he had never seen anything like it.

"It is called fire," Rukuba said, as if it were nothing at all.

"Who owns it?"

"My master, whose name is Fire God."

"And where," Nkhango wondered, "is your master now?"

"Away."

Rukuba drew nearer to the fire to warm himself.

"May I do that, too?" Nkhango asked.

Rukuba looked all around him. The tall grass quivered. The diamond dew twinkled. But Fire God was nowhere to be seen or felt. The world was at ease with itself, for the gods were elsewhere, having their earthly and heavenly council.

"You may warm yourself," Rukuba consented.

Nkhango got as close to the fire as he dared, for it touched his flesh with warmth and then bore all the way into his bones.

"When will your master return?" Nkhango said, rubbing his hands before the crackly light.

"Be careful," Rukuba warned. "The appetite of fire is endless."

Nkhango drew back. He felt the warmth on his skin spread quickly, and now it was like the sting of an insect.

"I see that it is so," he said, respectful of the dancing light.

And then a wonderful idea came to him. A thought full of power.

"I should like to have some of this fire for myself," Nkhango said.

Rukuba wrinkled his nose. He looked about him. The grass shivered, and quivered, and shone. The wind sighed, the sun swam, the day breathed deeply, and the trees exhaled.

"And if I should give you what you desire—" said Rukuba.

"I would reward you."

"How?"

"By taking care of you forever," Nkhango promised.

Rukuba liked this very much. His life was nothing but work—his time spent guarding, watching, looking about. And, always, feeding the fire. How Rukuba longed to be on his own. To be free from these never-ending duties. How he dreamed of someone taking care of him, of living a life of ease.

"If you take care of me forever, I will steal the fire for you. I will bring it to your place, and there we two shall live in peace for the rest of our lives."

Now, in three days' time, Rukuba came to Nkhango and he brought with him a small black urn, which swung to and fro as he walked. The urn smoked because it contained fire coals.

Nkhango was pleased when he saw the smoking urn. "You have done as you said, my friend."

Rukuba, however, hung his head in shame. "I have paid dearly for your gift," he said.

Nkhango's eyes were fixed on the urn. "Hmm," he mumbled, looking only at the winking embers.

"You will see what I mean when you pour the fire coals onto the earth. Then my punishment begins."

Entranced, Nkhango was still not listening. He took the urn excitedly and poured the coals onto the earth. The fire sprang up, clapping its hands, demanding its food of wood.

Nkhango grinned. "Now, what did you say, my friend?" he asked, looking at Rukuba for the first time.

But Rukuba said nothing, for he could no longer speak. That gift, the presence of speech, was now taken from him. Fire God had made it so: It was the punishment for Rukuba's theft.

However, Nkhango felt sorrow for his new friend. And since he had promised to always take care of him, Nkhango made a collar for Rukuba, to make up for the dog's missing voice. He used wet antelope skin into which he placed a handful of thorns. When the antelope skin collar dried, Nkhango put it around Rukuba's neck, and the collar made a pretty noise.

"There, you can speak," Nkhango told Rukuba.

And, when Rukuba nodded, the little thorn-bells rang like rain on the leaves of the trees.

Now, when the two friends went hunting together, Nkhango always knew where Rukuba was because he could hear his collar ringing when Rukuba jumped up in the grass. And that is why the basenji is called the African Barkless Dog, or, sometimes, the Jumping-Up-Dog, because he loves to jump up and make the little bells ring like the fourth morning of the world.

AFTERWORD

The dogs of African gods are too numerous to name. There are—to cite only a few—the dogs of Dahomey, the dogs of Fjort, and the dogs of Yoruba. All of these are sacred figures, creation animals who have helped humankind "in the beginning." As such, these ancestor dogs are considered "culture heroes"; that is, they were our first teachers and they instructed our foreparents in the ways of the world.

The tale of Nkhango and Rukuba comes from the Nyanga people of the Belgian Congo. Here, Dog is the bestower of fire and the cocreator of the dog-bell that exists to this day as the common collar.

The basenji, an African breed, resembles Rukuba. Used as a hunter, this tough, compact dog was known as the African Barkless and the Congo Dog. He was also called the Jumping-Up-Dog for the way he leaped into the air to gain height over the tall African grasses. In the Congo region, the Basenji was employed to hunt twenty-pound reed rats. In his role as the African Barkless, he spoke not a word—as the legend tells us. However, upon his first appearance at a dog show in England, he contradicted his own history—he yodeled.

The Trickster Dog

Why Dogs Cannot Talk Like People: An Akita Tale

ONCE THERE WAS A DOG called First Dog, after which there were the children of First Dog, and then the grandchildren of First Dog, and so on and so forth, all the way to the present time.

Akita of Japan was First Dog's grandson, so they say—and he was there at the beginning of the world. In those first days of life, Akita could talk, as we talk now, which is to say, just like a person. However, with speech comes pride, and Akita did not like being talked down to, being told by people, "Do this, do that . . ." He did not like hearing the word "master," and he did not like being a slave.

All in all, because Akita was one of the firstborn of the earth, possessing speech and intelligence, no less than man or woman, he resented the position people had given him. In short, he wanted to be exactly like us. He wanted to be "top dog."

Now, the first human beings were hunter people, and Akita himself was a great hunter, too, one of the greatest that ever was, and First Hunter knew this and always took Akita along with him when he went out hunting. But, afterward, he would brag to First Hunter's Woman how he had made all the kills—so he, alone, got all the credit. Akita had to listen to First Hunter's lies around the fire at night; of how brave he was when he faced Bear, or how cleverly he tricked Lion.

One day, as it happened, Akita decided to set the record straight. He was tired of First Hunter getting all the credit, and Akita's heart was set against him.

So he told First Hunter, "Go into that thicket and kill what is there."

"What is hiding in there, Akita?" First Hunter asked. For he never went in first, but always second.

"Deer," Akita lied.

"Why don't you go in first, as is our custom?"

"I will wait out here, and if Deer bounds away, I will stop her escape."

So First Hunter agreed to this new tactic. He entered the thicket, and what he found there surprised him.

It wasn't Deer—it was Bear. And Bear killed First Hunter with one huge, crushing blow.

Akita said to himself, "So far, my plan is working out well. Now I'll go home and marry First Hunter's Woman." For that was his plan all along.

When First Hunter's Woman saw Akita come home by himself, she asked what had happened. Akita told her of the terrible way that Bear had surprised them, and how Akita had tried to save First Hunter, but he was too late.

"Such a thing never happened before," First Hunter's Woman said, her eyes filling with tears.

Akita licked his paws and looked innocently at First Hunter's Woman. "I told him not to enter the dangerous thicket where Bear was hiding. But he insisted on going in first. He said he knew Deer was in there. But it wasn't Deer, it was Bear. And Bear killed First Hunter. And that is all there is to it."

"What ever will I do now?" First Hunter's Woman asked the heavens.

Akita came close and put his paw around her. His curled-up tail was round as a moon shell.

"You shall be my wife now," he said confidently.

First Hunter's Woman glanced at Akita, and she wondered if he were telling her the truth. *Perhaps Akita has done something to my husband*, she thought.

Akita, who was too clever for his own good, caught the question in the woman's eyes, and he made his next lie more elaborate than the first.

"First Hunter's wish, as he lay in my arms, was that you should marry me."

"Is that so?" said the woman, her suspicions mounting. To busy herself and hide her face, she began to sweep the dirt in front of the lodge.

Akita felt that things were not going his way. So he tried yet another lie.

"First Hunter said, just before he died, that he loved me like a brother."

"Is that so?" she said. Her eyes stayed on the ground as she kept sweeping.

Akita went on boldly. "He wanted, above everything, that you and I should live together as Dog and Wife." And his dark eyes glittered with deceit.

At this, the woman could hear the lies no longer. She whisked the broom at Akita's face and got him with a mouthful of dirt. Choking, he tried to speak but the words were not there. Akita, as they say, had bitten the dust. He was not dead, but for once, silent.

And so it is today: Akita still can't talk. Which is why, whenever given the chance, he digs in the dirt, trying to find his voice.

AFTERWORD

The Akita is sometimes called Akita-Ainu, meaning "sons of dogs," so this canine is a good candidate for First Dog. Excavations into the shell mounds of the Ainu, in the northernmost Japanese island of Honshu, reveal the remains of dogs and humans from prehistoric time. Therefore, the Akita, once used primarily as a fisherman's and hunter's dog, is a very old breed.

In the reign of the Japanese Emperor Yuryaku (A.D. 457–459), the Akita was a fighting dog, much as the bulldog was lord of the Westminster Pit in England. In time, the Akita, being the emperor's favorite, was entitled to special status. He wore a gold collar and traveled about on a golden throne. An elite language was devised in which to speak with royal Akitas, and ownership was not permitted outside the court. Today, the Akita is a national treasure of Japan, and the dog is so highly trusted as a family member that children are sometimes left at home with only an Akita in attendance. There is a statue of an Akita in a Tokyo railway station in honor of the dog who waited for his master's return many years after the man's death.

The Akita in our tale is true to form. Akitas, as a rule, do not bark on the hunt, and their silence is considered a great virtue. The Ainu, the aboriginal people of Japan, believe that the union of Dog and Woman formed their ancestors. The Akita in our story fails to take a human wife because he is a trickster. Yet his attempt earned him the honor of silence, his blessing as a hunter.

This story occurs in some form from India to the Ainus of Honshu and from southern Cameroon to the Hidatsas of North Dakota. It is as universal as speech and as honorable as silence.

How Dog Brought Death into the World: A Husky Tale

THE ESKIMOS SAY that Dog was created by Raven and his wife. Raven was not doing anything one day, and his wife said, "Raven, you are always bragging about how you stole the starlight and how you carry the moon on your back, and all such nonsense! Well, why don't you make something useful for a change?"

Raven thought about this. Then he said, "Once, as you know, I carved Killer Whale out of a piece of wood."

Raven's wife added, "Yes, and now he only catches fish for himself. He, too, is not useful. You should carve something we can use. Something as strong as Reindeer and as swift as Otter. Something that won't talk back the way our children do."

"Hmm," said Raven. "I think I see what it is you want."

All that day, Raven sat and thought about the thing he was going to make. He sat for a long time, and while doing so his fingernails grew long and curly and, because he was thinking about making something with four legs, a long snout, and a curly tail, those fingernails of Raven turned into Dog.

This happened sometime back in the beginning. Raven, at that time, knew the Creator-Of-All-Things better than the People did, who knew Him but a little. Soon Dog became great friends with the Creator, too.

One day, the Creator-Of-All-Things said, "Dog, I want you to do something for me. I cannot be going down to Earth all the time to show Man and Woman what is and what is not, so you must do that for me."

Dog nodded. "What do you want me to do?"

The Creator said, "I would like you to go down to Earth and show Man and Woman that there is no such thing as Death. Show them, for me, how it is possible to make a dead person become alive again. That way, they will know that life is everlasting."

Dog said he would do this, and he went down to Earth. But the first thing he saw was a woman wailing because her man had died.

The man was lying on his back with his arms stretched out and his eyes closed, but he was not sleeping; he was dead. So Dog went over to the woman and comforted her. After that, Dog forgot what he had promised to do for the Creator. He tried hard to remember, but the sight of the sorrowing woman made him forget. Besides, his memory was never very good to begin with. Dog asked himself, "Was I supposed to teach Woman how to bury Man? I believe that is what the Creator told me to do."

So, he showed Woman how a dead person was supposed to be buried and covered over with earth. But he told her it was the end and not the beginning. Woman helped with the burial. After which, she went back to the village and showed the People how to bury the dead. Everyone was glad of learning this new thing, and Dog went back up to the Creator and said, "I have done what you asked me to do."

The Creator, however, was angry with him.

"Dog, you have done a bad thing. You have shown men that it is all right to die and you have shown women how to bury them. But worst of all, you have given Death a big part of the world we made. That is bad, very bad."

"Oh," said Dog, sighing and making woo-roo noises in his throat, which he always did when he was sad.

"I see that I forgot what I was sent to do, woo-aroo-woo."

"You are so forgetful," said the Creator.

"Woo-aroo," cried Dog.

And, today, the husky still goes woo-aroo when he is feeling forgetful, which is most of the time. But he especially woo-aroos when it snows, and on nights when the moon is round with the memory of how things got to be the way they are.

AFTERWORD

The name husky comes from a corruption of the word "Eskimo," for these North American Indians created the husky by breeding a rugged dog with a timber wolf. This explains the husky's extraordinary temperament, both courageous and cautious. No dog has more stamina. The animated epic Balto *(Universal Pictures, 1995) was based on the true story—and, perhaps, an actual husky—of the 1925 Serum Run, in which husky sled dogs hauled medicine from Nenana to Nome, Alaska, during an outbreak of diphtheria. They went through minus fifty-degree blizzards, traveling over 650 miles in 127½ hours, to deliver the goods and save the lives of many children. The yearly Iditarod Sled Dog Race in Alaska is a re-creation of the famous Serum Run.*

The Siberian Eskimos believe that Dog was created by Raven and his wife. Dog's indestructible physique came from Raven's unbreakable toenails, the myth says. Another similar tale tells that Dog was first carved out of wood by the Creator. The Siberian Eskimos of Unisak, in the Bering Strait, say that this fine dog carries in him the spirit-heart of a tree; that is, the inexhaustible grain of wood rather than flesh. And this, they explain, is why the dog can outlast pain, cold, and other privations.

First Man and First Woman's Dog: A Coyote Tale

IN THE BEGINNING, the first beings were all friends. They worked together to make the world, if not better, at least brighter; because it was very dark in the beginning. In fact, it was pitch-patch black. And the animal people and the two-legged people and the insect people kept bumping into one another.

First Man and First Woman were there, however, to make things better. They had help, too, from the one called Coyote. He was always around, at that time, poking his nose into things. He stole Water Monster's two children, if you remember: He tucked them up under his arm and walked away with them. That made Water Monster so mad, she caused the Great Flood.

Yet, after all was said and done, the Great Flood was good because it pushed the People—animals, two-leggeds, and insects—up through a hollow reed into the next world, the world of light. There, things were not so dark, but still, it was hard to see, and the People stumbled around much of the time.

First Man then told the People to put some offerings on Bat's wings. This they did, scattering little bits of bright-colored corn pollen all over them. And Bat fluttered up into the heavens, and the offerings on his wings became the stars;

19

but they still did not shine. They barely glittered, even though Bat stayed up there for a time, polishing them with his darting little wings.

Then, First Woman said to First Man, "I think we had better do something else because it is still too dark to see and those stars up there are not bright enough."

First Man called forth the two Pollen Boys, for they could sing very sweetly. "We will have them sing the stars into being alive," First Man explained. So the Pollen Boys started to sing, but no song came from them.

"What mischief is this?" First Woman asked, thinking she already knew.

"Come over here, Coyote," First Man ordered. He discovered that Coyote had stolen the voices of the Pollen Boys, so their song had no sound.

Coyote felt ashamed of himself now because he had done two bad things: He had stolen Water Monster's children, which made the Great Flood, and he had taken the Pollen Boys' voices so the stars would not shine.

"I don't know why I do these bad things," Coyote confessed, "but I do them just the same."

"If you are as ashamed of yourself as we are ashamed of you, then you will fix what you have done." First Man chastised Coyote, who said he would make up for it.

He motioned to everyone. "Listen to me. I can sing as well as the Pollen Boys. I can polish stars just as well as Bat. I can make the world into a brighter place, you will see."

Then Coyote sang to the different directions, which was something altogether new. He sang to the east, to the south, to the west, and to the north. Then he gently breathed light into the stars. And, for the first time, they flickered. They glowed and, at last, burned.

"This is good," First Woman said. "We can prepare our food with such light. Coyote, you are not such a bad person after all."

Coyote received the praise of the People. He enjoyed being praised more than anything. He walked about with his chest puffed out and his tail flying high.

Then it was time to put up the Milky Way. First Man and First Woman arranged the constellations on a velveteen cloth spread upon the sand. Coyote, though, was still puffing about the camp, telling everyone what a fine thing he had done with the first rows of stars. But, now, as he was strutting self-importantly, he tripped and fell onto the constellation cloth—and the stars of the Milky Way spilled everywhere. They ran like white rivers into the sand. First Man and First Woman had to go around, gathering the rivers of stars. This time, they put them up in the heavens before Coyote could trip on them again.

Naturally, Coyote felt bad, but mostly, he just felt sorry for himself. The animal people and the two-leggeds got so tired of hearing Coyote's whining that they patted him on the back.

"You are still our friend," they said. "Just be

more careful where you put your hands and feet."

Coyote promised. Then he told them that he had many secret powers they did not know about.

"I am the one who will make rain when you plant corn," he explained. "And when babies are born, I will be there to help. And whenever you hear me cry out, you will know it is the end of day and the beginning of night; or the beginning of day and the end of night. I will be useful to you, you shall see."

In the days to come, Coyote "helped" with the sun and the moon and the gathering of the First Food known as Corn. But, try as he might, he could not help himself—once he stole the sun and burned his tongue. And he was very jealous of the moon, whose light was bright without his help.

Yet, in spite of those things, Coyote did prove himself useful, just as he promised. Selfish and foolish, he does what no other can.

Who but Coyote can call up the sun and chase away the dark? Who but Coyote falls off a cliff and sews himself back together with the thread of the wind? Who but Coyote has such names as Stink Breath, Baggy Pants, and First Angry? And who but Coyote makes you laugh until your sides hurt?

AFTERWORD

Coyote isn't a breed of dog. He is, however, the archetypal dog. No one knows when our relationship with coyotes began, but it must have been far back in our hunter-gatherer past. European storytelling traditions have mostly ignored this wily creature, the cousin of all domestic dogs. Yet Native Americans have made Coyote into a culture hero who is equal to any of their primary gods. In some stories there is the Creator and the great void of stars. The Creator extracts Coyote from His breast and casts him into the emptiness. Coyote then floats down to Earth and becomes the first animal person.

Most American Indian tribes have coyote tales. Usually, though, he is a master of misdeeds, an adventurer whose misadventures cause misfortune. However, as Coyote bumbles and stumbles through the first days of life, a valuable moral is taught. Coyote's errors—foolish and funny—have a positive outcome. The Navajos believe, for instance, that Coyote's mistakes brought about adaptations, which made the world a better place in which to live. This curious aspect of Coyote's behavior—doing bad things that turn out good—is celebrated in the Warner Brothers' "Wile E. Coyote" cartoons, which were originally influenced by American Indian myths.

The coyote tale that we have retold here was told to us by Navajo storyteller and artist Bluejay DeGroat of Crownpoint, New Mexico.

The Enchanted Dog

King Herla's Hound: A Bloodhound Tale

In THE LONG AGO, there lived a faery king of the Underground whose name was Redbeard. As it happened, the little king's best friend was Herla, the king of England. Often the two met and shared a flagon of fire-warmed wine and spoke of their great kingdoms, the one on top of the earth, and the other down below. There was, in truth, a cavern that linked the two worlds, which kept them together and apart.

"Come to my palace," the little king said one day to Herla. "You will not be disappointed."

"What does your kingdom have that mine does not?" asked Herla, who was of average size for an English monarch.

The little king thought for a moment. He sat, golden-saddled, upon a ram goat, his customary mount whenever he went about the upper regions of the daylight world.

"I will tell you, my dear friend," he said at last. "My kingdom has great cavernous halls with arches of emerald. The walls are fashioned of the finest beaten gold. Rivers run out of the rock, and we have fountains from which flow wine and glowing candles that float among the lotus flowers."

King Herla raised his eyebrows. "Have you more miracles of this sort?" he asked, incredulous.

The little king answered, "Come, and you shall see for yourself."

So King Herla mounted his horse and, with one hundred men, followed Redbeard to the mouth of the cave that led to the Underground. Into the cave went the little flame-faced king, riding upon his brown goat. And after followed King Herla and his legions of armored men.

When they entered the Underworld, there was much celebration. All the little people gathered round and toasted the tall people from the Up-Above. King Herla, his courtiers, and soldiers were much amazed at the finery of Redbeard's palace, a fiery, faery world, if ever there was one. All the little king had said was true: The Underground glittered with golden tracery, and the arches of emerald burned darkly in the halls.

Now, when it came time to leave, Redbeard presented Herla with a wonderful royal gift. It was a tiny hound dog, smaller than the palm of the Up-Above king. In truth, the hound was but two inches tall.

Amazed, King Herla announced, "I shall name him Herla's Hound."

Redbeard glowed with happiness. "Name him what you will," he said, "but mark you well. When you leave the

Underground, you must not dismount until your hound has set foot on the earth."

"A funny rule, that," said the grinning King Herla, "But I shall obey it just the same."

"Remember," the little king called as Herla started to leave, "set the dog down first!" His voice echoed in the gilded halls.

Then King Herla and his men rode upward toward the sun. Into the light the legion rose. And though they had been Underground just a fortnight, it seemed like a lifetime to them. The humpbacked hills gave the land the look of the sea, shimmering and shining. On they rode, admiring the world of day-bright light. Naturally, the king was in front, holding his hound on the flat of his open palm. The tiny dog stood with his ears drooping and his sad eyes surveying; in all ways except for size, he was a perfect bloodhound, a paragon of his breed.

Presently, they came to a crossroad where an old toothless man with a long white beard leaned upon a hazel walking stick.

"Hullo," King Herla greeted him.

The stranger looked at the armored men and the stamping horses and the odd kingly fellow with palm outstretched.

Squinting, he cried, "Who is coming in the clothes of some ancient land?"

"Look to," Herla commanded. "Do you not know who we are? It is I, Herla, your king, these are my men, and this noble dog is Herla's Hound."

The old man shook his head with disbelief. His snowy beard wagged in the sun. He swiveled this way and that, in confusion.

"I know not who you are, or wherefore you have come," he said, his voice trembling. "But by the look of you, sir, you're several hundred years too late—"

"Talk sense," Herla roared. "Your words outrun your reason." He was angry that this fool did not seem to know who he was—the king of England!

Scratching his bald head, the old man tried to explain.

"I once heard tell of some ancient king who disappeared without a trace. But that was just a lot of nonsense."

"What mad things you say," Herla hollered.

"I speak the truth," the stranger said meekly. Then he backed up, turned around, and began hobbling lamely down the road. When he felt he was a safe distance away, he shouted: "You are all an apparition, ghosts from another time."

"What fool's words his tongue does fashion," Herla said. "Does he still not know who I am?"

Herla felt it was time to beat sense into the man—and if anyone was going to do it, he would. In a rage, he jumped from his horse.

Suddenly, Herla's Hound vanished. Then his armored men flickered like spent flames in the sun and, with their horses still under them, they all snuffed out in the wind. After this, the king himself began to dissolve until his presence was nothing but a fog of smoke, and then, that, too, wound up and away and was gone. At last, nothing was there that was not there before: the oaks on the hills; the sun on high; the lame old man.

"I told them," he cried. "Ghosts, and they didn't even know it."

Now, the king and his men were never seen again. Some say they went back Underground. Others say they wander about to this very day, which explains the mournful cries that can still be heard in the hills of Northumberland on autumn nights. "That's Herla's Hound," people say, even though they know it's just the geese honking overhead as they fly south for the winter.

AFTERWORD

The story of Herla and his magic hound is an English myth, which, no doubt, has lineage in Celtic lore. Scottish faery dogs are also quite common in folklore. There is one tale about a faery hound named Favann, who, when in pursuit of quarry, barks three times. The third bark renders the fugitive frozen.

Such Highland legends feature faery dogs both good and bad. Our tiny bloodhound is one of the good ones, recalling the saying that "Mortals seldom prove worthy of a faery's trust." Hounds baying and geese honking refer, in the mythology of the British Isles, to lost souls searching for heaven or hell. In the oldest myths, these souls are trying to find the netherworld of the faery folk where life is everlasting.

Bloodhounds were called this name not because of their ferocity or tracking skill, but because of their royal breeding. These animals were originally bred by members of the French aristocracy. As the dogs owned by kings and queens, it is fitting that King Herla's bloodhound had something to do with the king's fate. Destiny and the bloodhound go well together. In the 1930s, in America, a bloodhound's "scent testimony" was worthy of a conviction in a court of law.

The Ghostly Weaver: A Retriever Tale

$\mathcal{A}$ LONG TIME AGO in the north of England, there was a workaday man, a weaver, who toiled all day long at his loom. From sunup to sundown, this man never got tired of treadling, treadling, treadling. Or pushing his shuttle with a shift and a shaggle, up and back, up and back.

Bickety, backety, crickety, crackety, his neighbors heard him weaving from miles away, and, oh, how their ears tired of the weaver's racket.

A farmer asked, "Why would a man spend his earthly days indoors making cloth when he could be out in the fields with his cows?"

Of course, the workaday weaver paid no mind to his neighbors. He just kept weaving all day long until the sun sank and the stars peeked. By then, he was too tired to weave anymore, and he went straight to bed.

However, when the sun rose, he was at it again: clickety, clackety, bickety, backety.

Now, it happened that one day this workaday man, this weaver, fell face first onto his loom and died. He had, it seemed, worked himself to death.

He was buried that same day.

And even the minister, who delivered the weaver's last rites, was relieved the man was gone. For his church was next door to that rattle-bang-clatter, and it racked his nerves to hear it. He and all the villagers gave a sigh of relief as the coffin was lowered into the ground.

Now the poor weaver, who had no family and, really, no friends, was dead and gone. And the town went on with its life—for the day, that is. However, that night, there came a cricky-cracky noise. Once again, a terrible racket poured out of the weaver's house.

In the morning the whole town was buzzing about it.

But the next night was even worse—the ghostly weaver was thundering and blundering. His loom crashed and bashed and made such an evil clamor that no one slept a wink. In the morning the townspeople complained to the minister. Surely this was the business of the church. Who but a minister could lay away the dead and make them quiet?

"Calm yourselves, people," the minister urged the villagers. "There shall be no more nights like last night. I will discipline the ghostly weaver. You can count on it."

So everyone went home, satisfied that something was going to be done. And that night, when the loom began to bang and the treadle tripped and sang, the minister

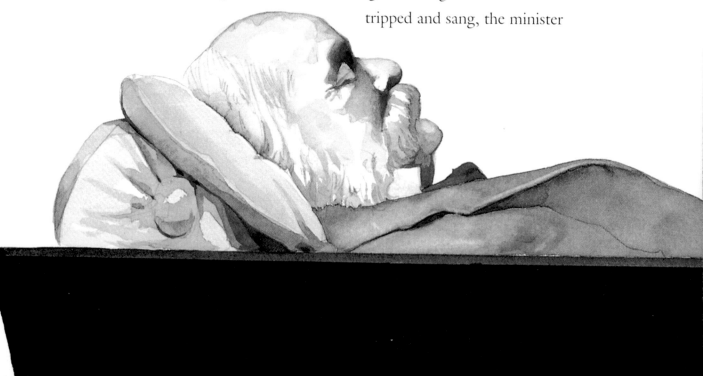

snuck up to the open window of the ghostly weaver's house.

What did he see?

Why, there was the ghostly weaver, of course, weaving cloth with a smile of spite on his lips.

"Hey, there," ordered the minister, "I want a word with you."

Fearlessly, he reached out and tapped the ghost on the shoulder, but his hand went right through to the other side.

Now what do I do? the minister wondered.

But the ghostly weaver kept to his work. The minister went home.

What is it that ghosts are afraid of? he asked himself. Outside in the pale milky light, he saw the cemetery. The neat rows of separate graves with their white crosses at the top gave him an idea. He got his Bible and a handful of graveyard dirt, and he walked back to the ghostly weaver's house.

This time, the minister stood at an open window where the moonlight lay like spun cotton. He called the ghostly weaver forth. "Sir," said the minister, "don't you know the whole village is trying to get some sleep?"

The ghostly weaver paid him no mind.

"Sir," he said again, "do you not have anything else you could do?"

The ghostly weaver paid him no mind.

Now the third time the minister called forth the ghostly weaver, he said to the discourteous spirit, "Sir, what if all the souls who have been put to rest on this earth were to return to their former work?"

Still, the ghostly weaver paid him no mind.

So, the minister reached into his right-hand coat pocket and produced the handful of graveyard dirt and, forthwith, he threw it into the face of the ghostly weaver. All at once, the weaver changed into a large, black curly-coated retriever.

The minister smiled. The moon shone pleasantly upon the fields of newly planted corn, and, at last, the whole town slept with contentment.

However, as the minister went home, smiling, the curly-coated retriever padded along after him, down the moonlit path; and the dog smiled, too. Presently, the minister arrived at his doorstep and so did the big, hearty dog, whose curls stood like links of iron in the moonlight.

"Come here, dog," the minister called.

The curly-coated retriever did as he was bidden.

The minister bent down and picked up an acorn shell. "I want you to take this shell and bale out the pond over yonder. I want you to have it done by tomorrow morning. Do you hear me, dog?"

The curly-coated retriever wagged his tail three times, which meant that he understood the minister's command.

"Very well," said the minister, chuckling. Then, using his penknife, he punched a hole in the shell and handed it to the eager dog, who took it in his mouth and trotted toward the pond.

Bail, bail, bail. Swish, swash, swish. All night long that dog tried to empty the pond of water—but, of course, he could not do it. For, as soon as he had the acorn full of water, it spilled out of the hole. And so, back he went to try again. . . .

They say that the curly-coated retriever is at it to this day. He bails and pours, bails and pours. But no matter how hard he tries, he cannot do such an impossible thing as empty a pond with a leaky acorn shell.

And it's not just because he's a ghost—for did you ever know a retriever who gave up going after something? The chase is the thing, even more than the capturing.

Well, that is how a workaday man became a ghostly weaver, who was then changed into a curly-coated retriever, who, some say, is still a weaver, with threads of moon water hanging from his chin.

AFTERWORD

This tale is a standard in the ghost dog métier. Dogs, in many of our favorite myths, have sight beyond the grave. Moreover, those canines who have passed beyond the pale come back to haunt the living. Their reason for doing this? It would seem that dog ghosts are a kind of conscience, reminding us of something we've forgotten to do. In our story, the weaver works too hard at his trade, and his dog ghost, or other self, comes back to tell him, "What you do lives after you." In more ways than one, we might add.

The curly-coated retriever loves being in, or around, water. This canine is related to the poodle and is one of the oldest of duck dogs. Although not well known in America, he is respected in England, and, if one were to assign such a task as bailing out a pond, experts say the curly-coated retriever would not quit until the job was done.

The Guardian Dog

Prince Llewelyn's Gelert: A Wolfhound Tale

IN THE TIME OF THE feudal lords, in Wales, there lived a prince named Llewelyn, who had a beloved wolfhound named Gelert. Together, across the leafy glens and through the piney woods, the two traveled, hunters each, with the love of the hunt bred in their bones. Many was the time they sat on a highland hill, Llewelyn tilting his wineskin to the sun while his faithful Gelert chewed on a pinecone at his feet. However, the day came when all of this would change.

It happened in the following way.

The prince left early one morning to hunt a pack of marauding wolves. Gelert, as usual, was ever at his side. Shaggy-browed and misty as a wolf, Gelert stood six hands high, and his harsh, wiry fur was like chain mail all about him. As the two went out together, they looked, for the life of them, like brothers—but for the two legs of the one and the four legs of the other.

They trailed the wolf pack into the forested mountains that surrounded the stone house of the prince. "No more lambs will these beasts steal, eh, Gelert?"

Sniffing the wind, the great gray Gelert seemed to nod at the prince's words. Then, the gallant dog suddenly took to the chase. "You've seen one, then—" the prince cried out. And he ran to catch up to his dog—yet he might have tried to catch the wind. Gelert, as was his wont, vanished into the thick wood.

Prince Llewelyn followed. But he never quite caught up. Always the grayish cloud ahead of him garlanded some new vista, and was gone. "If I cannot see you, I cannot catch up to you," the prince said, all out of breath. And then he saw his mistake. A huge-shouldered wolf ran in front of him. It was not Gelert he was chasing, but the leader of the wolf pack. Realizing his error—and knowing that he was far from home and without his dog—Llewelyn retreated. He retraced his footsteps and, in time, came to the place where his stone manor stood against the pines. Still, no sign of Gelert.

Now strange thoughts ran through the prince's mind. Exhausted from his run, he envisioned terrible things.

Gelert, left all alone in the wilderness, killed by the numberless wolves. Or, wounded, dragging himself through the bracken. Then, Llewelyn saw a horrible sight. The oval entryway of his stone house was dark, his door wide open. Hastening across the open field that led to his home, the prince burst through the open doorway, sword in hand.

There, in the corner of the hall, was a rumpled bear rug and the overturned cradle of his son. Blood was everywhere, puddled like spilled wine.

Then, out of the dark corner, came Gelert grinning with red-rimmed mouth.

Now, thinking his dog had killed his son, the prince plunged his sword into Gelert's heart. At the same time, he heard an infant's cry from underneath the cradle and caught sight of the torn shape of a dead wolf, in the shadow of the hall.

Beneath the overturned cradle, safe as could be, was his son. He picked up the boy and saw there was not a scratch on him. Carefully, Llewelyn put the cradle upright and placed his son into it. Then he looked at his dog.

"What have I done?" the prince cried, sinking to his knees. He cradled the head of Gelert as hot tears coursed his cheeks.

"I have slain the most faithful companion a man ever had," Llewelyn said. But there was nothing he could do to bring his best friend back to life. It was too late. Through a mist of tears, Llewelyn said:

"One thing I promise you, my beloved Gelert. Each year, in the season of flowers, I will bring you a hillside of blossoms. And I shall build you a tomb, such as no dog ever had, so that your memory will live on forever."

True to his word, the prince built a turreted tomb for his dog under a huge basswood tree. Each year, when the larks filled the clouds with song, he made good his promise. Arms full of daisies and barley, he came to offer his prayers to the best dog that ever lived.

This is how the village of Beddgelert came to be named. In Welsh, it means "Gelert's Grave," and if you should go there, you would hear the proverb, known throughout the world, "To repent as deeply as the man who killed his dog."

AFTERWORD

The Gelert tale has been called "the most famous dog story ever told." Perhaps this is because it is based on a true happening in the thirteenth century. The folktale also contains many elements of fine storytelling. It is not only about irony and penance, but about seeing things truly and not being deceived. Best friends, for example, remain so because of the deep faith they hold for one another. Prince Llewelyn's failure to believe fully in his dog's trustworthiness shows a weakness in his own character, one that is often thought to be a "human weakness." Certainly dogs, in general, do not lack faith in us.

Wolfhounds are noble, full of wisdom and compassion for those whom they love. Yet, all in all, they are most famous for their ferocity. The Gaelic saying goes, "Gentle when stroked, fierce when provoked." As a breed they appeared in Rome (A.D. 391) at the Imperial Circus. Later, they were decorated on the fighting fields of Ireland, and they feasted in the feudal castles of Wales.

The first job of the wolfhound—and the reason for its name—was to hunt down the marauding packs of wolves that roamed the British Isles. But after the wolves were nearly hunted to extinction, the dogs themselves began to disappear. Breeders brought them back again in the nineteenth century, and they hunted wolves once again on the plains of the American West.

The Seven Sleepers: A Saluki Tale

THERE WAS ONCE a cruel war in the desert of Arabia, in which seven faithful young men fled for their lives. They took leave of their homes in haste and, as the Roman legions swept through their town, these seven youths disappeared into the starry folds of the desert night. Walking barefoot until dawn, they collapsed on the sand and slept.

As they lay there, the wind came up and rustled around them, but still they slept on. The wind blew scarves of sand over them and erased their footprints. And they slept on.

Finally, the eldest boy awoke and said, "Look, the desert is changed—"

"That will not stop the Roman army," said his friend. "They will soon come to kill us, for we are the only ones left from our village."

Now the seventh youth surveyed the desert sands. He saw the dunes like white leaven, like the unbaked bread of heaven. White, hot. And the oven of the sun growing hotter all the time.

"So," said the seventh, "have you not felt the blessing of this place? We are safe here."

As he said this, a sleek dog, a saluki, appeared upon the dunes, trotting toward them. The dog was handsomely built with farseeing eyes set in a narrow, tapered head. Deep-chested, long-legged, the dog made her way to the astonished seven.

"A miracle," said the seventh youth.

"Truly, it is so," the first affirmed.

The alert, feather-tailed dog looked up, searching the faces of the youths to make sure they were all there. Then she trotted to a hill of sand. There, she whined until the young men came to her and spoke soothingly. But she would not be comforted.

She dug at the sand, and the hill began to melt, and it

started to flow like water. A secret cave lay behind the sparkling sand dune, and this was what the saluki was after.

Now the seven youths went into the coolness of the cave. Outside, the sun sliced down the sky like a golden blade. Slowly, the youths sank to their knees and soon a deep slumber fell upon them, and they slept again.

And slept.

For 309 years, they say, the seven youths continued to sleep. Anyone who tried to awaken them was struck by a burning wind.

And, all the while, their patient guardian, the saluki, with her paws stretched across the entrance of the cave, watched over them. She never left her post, not even for the temptation of food. And yet, this magic dog had no need of anything to replenish her spirit. For she, as everyone knows, was immortal.

When the seven youths finally awakened, their persecutors were gone. The world was not at war. Some say, however, that the trusted saluki then took the seven sleepers to paradise, where they still live.

And that is why the sleek saluki is called *el hor,* "the noble one." And it is also why the Bedouin call a greedy person "one who would not throw a bone to the dog of the seven sleepers."

AFTERWORD

The Seven Sleepers myth is Muslim, Christian, and Jewish. In most versions of the tale, the savior dog is present. In the Koran it is stated: ". . . they tarried in their Cave three hundred years and add nine" (Sûrah XVIII, 26). In Christian mythology, the story places the seven youths outside the city of Ephesus on the coast of Asia Minor at around A.D. 750. Our version combines elements of all these desert cultures. We have highlighted the saluki as a teacher of courage, patience, cunning, and faith.

It is also one of the oldest dog breeds on Earth; Sumerian and Egyptian murals and carvings 5,000 years old feature the lithe saluki figure. Originating in the Arabian town of Saluk, from which the dog gets its name, this breed is said to possess magic. Among the Mohammedans of Morocco, the saluki is the essence of baraka—*the mysterious, supernatural power invested in such things as brides-to-be, camels, and mountains. The dog's telescopic sight is thought to be the gift of Allah. Bedouin hunters say, "The saluki can catch a gazelle, even if the gazelle should jump over the moon."*

One final note must be added here. Yet another reason why the saluki is in a class by itself is the fact that the sleek saluki is not considered to be a dog by Muslims. Dogs are thought to be unclean, but the saluki is so pure that he may eat out of a sheik's personal food dish.

The Thunder Mouth Dog: A Rottweiler Tale

THE GREAT GOD THOR was stronger and smarter than any of the other gods of the Scandinavian North. But even he could be tricked. Once, while Thor was asleep on a hunting trip, a giant named Thrym stole his hammer—a weapon forged from a thunderbolt. Now, although Thor might be fooled and, on occasion, overcome by force, with hammer in hand, he was invincible. The power of his mighty hammer was such that he could hurl it like lightning, and where it struck, destruction would flower.

"I want my hammer back," Thor told Thrym. "Is there anything you will trade for it?"

"I will return your hammer only after I have married the goddess Freyja," Thrym said. "Do not come after me, Thor, for I'll kill you with your own hammer."

Thor, strong as he was, could not defeat a crazed giant who possessed such a powerful weapon.

I must think of a way to trick Thrym, Thor thought.

Soon, a plan lay itself before him. First, he dressed himself in the skirts of Freyja. Then, donning a white blouse with blue and green trim, he threw a red cloak over his shoulders. The golden ringlets of his shoulder-length hair hung down, but so did Freyja's, so the disguise was perfect. Thor's red face and rusty beard were the only giveaways; yet these he hid under a veil that covered all but his eyes. Another giant might have seen through this trickery. However, poor, stupid Thrym was not only desperately in love, he was a bit nearsighted as well.

With his trusty Rottweiler, Thunder, for company, Thor made his way to Thrym's castle, arriving at nightfall. He knocked on the door and heard the echoes of distant footfalls within. The door swung wide, and Thrym bellowed, "Who stirs there in the foulness of the night?"

Thunder raised his hackles, showing ivory-white teeth. Here was the world's toughest guardian, a dog sculpted squarely, as if out of blocked stone. Yet Thunder knew when to close in and when to be still. Growling, he quieted under Thor's calm hand.

"I say, who goeth?" the giant repeated loudly, regarding the dog with disdain.

"It is I, your betrothed," squeaked Thor, pretending to be the goddess Freyja.

"Is it—indeed?" quaked the surprised giant.

"Very cold am I, Your Giantness," said Thor. "I have journeyed far to be at your side on this, our wedding night. I am cold, hungry, and very thirsty."

"Such words you use." Thrym chuckled. "Come inside at once, but leave your dog behind."

"I cannot do that," said Thor. "Thunder here guided me through rain and storm, ambush and night; he's my most faithful friend."

"Bring yourselves both in, then."

Thrym escorted the well-disguised Thor and his broad-chested,

soft-footed dog into a monstrous hall, before which there roared a fire with full-grown trees burning in it. Thunder lay down before the flames, but he kept his eyes wide open.

Thor, seeing the table spread with food, began to drool. It dripped off his chin and onto his shirtfront. In the firelight, Thrym's quick eye saw this.

"What is that I see?"

"Why, nothing, dearest," Thor said sweetly. "It's just the rain from the wet night dripping off my chin."

"Stand by the fire so I can have a better look at you," the giant ordered suspiciously.

Thor did as he was told, and Thrym stared, eyes glowing with desire. He had never seen such a broad-shouldered, stoutly built woman. The more he looked at her, the more he liked her rough-hewn features. "You are more lovely than ever." The giant sighed. "Now please remove your veil so I may feast upon your beauty."

"No, my love," Thor said. "Not until I have eaten and my belly is full."

"Is this how women talk?" Thrym wondered aloud. He scratched the wart on his chin. Then Thor turned toward the vast array of meats, fishes, and breads, and began to eat. By bringing his food under the veil that covered his face, he kept his identity a secret. However, in no time, he had swallowed eight whole salmon and an entire ox, throwing the bones to Thunder, who ground them up with his teeth. After this, Thor quaffed three barrels of beer sweetened with honey. Then, forgetting himself, he wiped his chin. The veil slipped aside, revealing a tuft of beard.

Thrym's eyebrows went up several times during the meal as he watched Thor clean the table of food, but now he said, "Woman, you eat like a man—no, worse, like a god!"

Quickly Thor replied, "My hunger's nothing compared to my love for you."

"Something's wrong here," Thrym declared, eyeing Thor.

Then he jumped from the table, snatching away Thor's veil.

"I see something," the giant roared. "You have much hair on your face."

Thunder dropped a bone and growled from across the room, but Thor stilled him with a glance.

"Yes, Your Giantness," Thor said, blushing, and he batted his eyes at Thrym.

"I've never known a woman with a beard," Thrym said.

"Have you never seen a goddess this close?"

"Nay," said the giant.

"Then how do you know they do not have beards?"

"I don't," said Thrym.

"If we are to be married," Thor chirped, "you must bring out the hammer—as is our custom."

Thrym strode across the room to the chest where he kept his things. Inside it was Thor's magic hammer. Thrym took it out and said, "When I place this hammer on your knees, we shall be husband and wife."

Thor's eyes danced when he saw his weapon.

Then Thrym dragged his chair over to Thor, and the two sat side by side. Thrym placed Thor's hammer on the god's knees. Whereupon Thor seized it, raised it high, and brought it down upon the head of Thrym.

Immediately, the giant fell dead on the floor.

Thor threw off his disguise and was himself again.

Then he called Thunder and said, "From this time on, you shall always carry my weapon in your mouth to keep it from thieving hands."

And the great dog did as he was told, which is why, today, Rottweilers growl more fiercely than any other watchdog. For they believe they are still holding on to Thor's hammer. That is why one cannot take anything away from them. And it is also why their growl sounds like thunder in their throat.

AFTERWORD

The old German god of thunder and war was named Donar, and he was revered by all the Teutonic tribes. But in certain northern countries, particularly Norway, the same god was known only as Thor. In fact, the name in the northlands was interchangable—Donar/Thor.

Norse poets have depicted Thor as a noble warrior, a hero without peer, the victor of all giants and demons. Naturally, his dog had to be an invincible warrior as well, reflecting the mythic qualities of his master.

Visible in medieval paintings, the Rottweiler also appears in the tales of Siegfried and Odin. The blocky, muscular Rottweiler, which is descended from the Molossian mastiff of Tibet, is perhaps the watchful descendant of Thunder.

The name Rottweiler is derived from the German town of Rottweil, which means "red tile." Originally, these dogs drove cattle to market. They belonged to the drover-butchers, whose practice was to have the dog carry a change purse about its neck. No highwayman would dare challenge the most ferocious of all watchdogs, the Rottweiler.

Proof of Thor's hammer being protected by a dog is shown in an Icelandic chair made in the Middle Ages. The carved arm of the chair features a dog's head. In its mouth is the fabled hammer. "Beware," the chair seems to say, "who enters this house is watched by Thor's dog, Thunder."

The Super Dog

A Dog Named Boye: A Poodle Tale

THERE WAS ONCE an English prince named Rupert, who had an amazing and wonderful white poodle named Boye. Never was there a dog like Boye, and there probably never will be again.

Now, Rupert and Boye were Cavaliers, which means, among other things, that they wore long, shoulder-length wigs, as was the royal custom. But this wasn't the only hairstyle of the time. There were Roundheads, too, so called because they wore their hair so short, you could see their bony heads.

There was a war going on between the Cavaliers and the Roundheads, and it wasn't about the way to wear one's hair. The Cavaliers liked the king, Charles I; the Roundheads didn't. The Cavaliers liked Prince Rupert and his white poodle, Boye; the Roundheads didn't. Neither party liked spinach, but that is another story.

Yet why, do you suppose, the Roundheads didn't like Prince Rupert's dog, Boye? What reason could there possibly be?

Well, how many dogs do you know that can speak Hebrew and High Dutch? Boye could speak each tolerably well, and he could also speak English and French. Yet that wasn't the reason the Roundheads feared Boye. It was the business about him being able to change his shape and spy on people.

You see, Boye enjoyed sneaking up on Roundheads and reporting what they said to Prince Rupert, who would then go to the king. Boye, the shape-shifter, could turn himself into Philip, the Shoemaker, who, being out on the street a lot, picked up all the latest gossip.

Boye also liked to change himself into Tom, the Barber; or Bill, the Bookbinder. Because Tom trimmed the Roundheads' heads, he picked up all the news there was. However, Bill also heard lots of gossip. One day, when Boye turned himself into Bill, he overheard some Roundheads saying they were going to throw mud at Prince Rupert when he walked to church on Sunday.

So, when Sunday rolled around, Boye, who was white to begin with, turned into a fleecy cloud and hung himself right over Rupert's head. Now, everyone was wondering where the pretty cloud had come from when out came the Roundheads with their hands full of sticky-gooey mud. And they started slinging it at Prince Rupert and his fellow Cavaliers. Some of the mud balls had rocks in them, and they knocked the Cavaliers down. For a while, it really looked like the Roundheads were getting the better of Prince Rupert.

"How dare they do this on a Sunday!" the prince cried.

Then did Boye rise up, cover the sun, and fire hail upon the mudslinging men, scattering them on the spot.

One of the Roundheads shouted, "This dog is no dog."

Another Roundhead, while shielding his head from hail, said, "This dangerous Cavalier dog's got the Devil in him."

And so it was that the Roundheads began to plot a way to destroy Boye.

First, they fired lead balls at Boye with their
pistols, but Boye caught the bullets in his teeth and
saved them for the prince. Then the Roundheads tried
to throw a net over him, but Boye changed himself into a
snake and wriggled away. Finally, at the Battle of Marston
Moor, a Roundhead, who told everyone he was a magician, snuck up
behind Boye as he was fighting alongside the prince and killed him with a
silver bullet.

Yet, no sooner did Boye fall upon the field of battle than a white cloud
rose up into the sky. It was broad as a sailing ship and it had a great bow
and a fine stern, and it floated cleanly over the sea-blue sky.

"That's no ship," Prince Rupert cried. "It's Boye!" And the huge cloud
drifted over that battlefield, casting fear into many a Roundhead heart.

Some say that Boye died on the battlefield that day, struck down by the
silver bullet. They say the Roundheads found a magician, like Merlin, who
fired the deadly shot. Well, it did happen that the Roundheads won the
Battle of Marston Moor. But there are those who believe that Boye wasn't
killed—that, once again, he turned into a cloud and disappeared into the
sky. You can see him today, some people say. There, in that fluffy, puffy,
ever scruffy, poodle-headed cloud.

AFTERWORD

The poodle was once considered the dog of all seasons. A dog who was comfortable in any climate, doing any sort of thing. Today, our image of the poodle has changed. For instance, Walt Disney Productions (Oliver & Company, among other animated films) presents the poodle as a fussy female, a dog of wealth and whimsy. Yet this ultimate retriever, the all-season poodle, was far from finicky in the days of the classic duck hunt.

The poodle's French name was originally chien canne, or "duck dog." However, the word "poodle" comes from the German pudeln, which means "to splash about in the water," something the breed is famous for. This dog's fur, in fact, is almost watertight and was grown especially thick at the joints for extra warmth—not for fashion, as people so often imagine.

Boye is the earliest recorded poodle to be known by name. He was first described in an English parliamentary broadsheet in 1642 at the time of the English Civil War. Broadsheets, or broadsides, were single-page, hand-printed texts of poetry, story, news, or political messages, which were passed out freely on the streets of London. This real dog was probably of such virtue to his master, Prince Rupert, that a comical writer decided to use him for literary purposes. He was thus described as a "metamorphosis dog," a "dogge of changes." In writer's magic, Boye became a shape-shifter of sorts. But we know the truth. This true-to-life dog is the plain old pudeln, whose natural behavior is most supernatural.

The Dog Who Married a Princess: A Shar-pei Tale

*F*OUR THOUSAND YEARS AGO, Emperor Kao-hsin of China offered a portion of his kingdom to anyone who could defeat his archenemy, the wicked sorcerer Wu. None but the bravest dared face Wu, who combined the skills of a martial artist with the craft of a magician.

"Such an evil man," said Kao-hsin, "is not easily taken."

"What you must do," said his daughter, whose name was Yun-ch'i, "is hire someone who is capable of capturing Wu."

"I have already searched the kingdom for such a man," said the emperor.

"You must offer a treasure more precious than gold or land."

"What could that be, my child? There is only one thing more precious than my kingdom—and that is you."

Then the emperor clapped his hands together. "That's it!" he cried. "I shall offer your hand in marriage to the one who can defeat our old enemy, Wu."

Yun-ch'i nodded. Her father was her lord; whatever he said was the law.

So, the emperor's decree was posted all over the kingdom.

And no one noticed when Pan-Hu, the great, wrinkled, sand-colored dog,

who lived in the palace and was a
guardian there, went off to seek his
fortune. In fact, Pan-Hu knew
exactly what he was doing. As a
fighter he had no equal. He was,
in addition, wise and kind. And
there was no one in the palace he
adored more than Yun-ch'i. For he
had guarded the princess ever since
she was a babe in arms. Now he went
out to do battle with the wicked Wu.

Pan-Hu, the wrinkled one, was no
fool. He padded straight to Wu's castle in
the Jade Mountains and, begging entry with
a bark, was admitted. No one knew where

the great dog had come from, but a fighting dog of Pan-Hu's size was worth fifty men. He was broad at the shoulder, huge at the head, yet he walked as softly as a cat. Soon Pan-Hu was made a member of Wu's elite fighting corps.

Then, one night, while Wu was sleeping, Pan-Hu took him by surprise and killed him.

Afterward, when Pan-Hu returned to the kingdom of Kao-hsin, he brought with him the head of Wu. The emperor could not believe that a dog had beaten a human sorcerer of Wu's stature, but the people chanted, "Pan-Hu, Pan-Hu," and they made a hero of the dog. However, the emperor had no desire to give his daughter away to a wrinkly canine. So, although he praised Pan-Hu publicly and gave him the gold and the land, he declined to give over Yun-ch'i.

"My Lord," Yun-ch'i said softly, "Pan-Hu has done what you asked, and you must give him my hand in marriage. It is what you promised, and the only honorable thing to do."

In truth, Yun-ch'i believed that Pan-Hu was wiser and kinder than most men. Certainly, he was braver. What did it matter that he was four-legged rather than two-legged? He was neither deceitful nor boastful. Moreover, she believed he would actually make a good husband. Everyone knows that a dog loves with his whole heart, and Yun-ch'i had felt Pan-Hu's devotion ever since she could remember. So, now, she returned this love with the bond of matrimony.

Happily, Pan-Hu carried his bride on his big, strong back. He took her to the mountains of the South, where they lived together in a cave and raised twelve children. Today, four thousand years later, Pan-Hu is remembered at the turning of the New Year. In the temples of Yunto in Szechuan, Pan-Hu is considered the great ancestor dog, and legend tells that some people there still have tails.

AFTERWORD

Shar-pei, which means "sand dog" in Chinese (for the coarse-grained, sandy-feeling fur), is a breed possibly dating back to the late Han Dynasty (206 B.C. to A.D. 220). Herding, guarding, and hunting dogs, Shar-peis were a mixture of Chow, Great Pyrenees, and Tibetan mastiff. They were well known in China as fighting dogs, and their appearance supported this claim. Their toes, for instance, were always slightly turned out, which was said to improve their balance, poise, and strength. This characteristic was also thought to resemble the mythical Chinese Crawling Dragon, with feet pointing east and west.

Our story happened during the reign of Emperor Kao-hsin (2435–2366 B.C.), when his realm was under attack by a war chief named Wu, who was a member of the Chuan-jung tribe. The story concludes with Pan-Hu and his bride living happily ever after, but there is a postscript to the tale. Pan-Hu, great though he was, was mortal. After he died, presumably of old age, the princess returned to her father's court. However, her six daughters and six sons were miserable there. Country born and bred, they wanted to roam freely. Finally, they were permitted to go home to the windy hills, where they married one another and had many descendants, all of whom were exempt from paying taxes because of the service Pan-Hu once rendered the emperor.

Stories where human beings marry dogs are widely spread throughout the world. North American Indian tales often feature such marriages, sometimes with Coyote, the trickster, who was considered a god-dog. Generally, such myths are called dog ancestor tales. Yet, in this case, the dog becomes a superhero when he defeats a human enemy to marry a princess.

The Treasure Dog

The Dog, the Cat, the Snake, and the Ring: A Bichon Frise Tale

*T*HERE WAS ONCE a boy named Theodore, who lived on the Mediterranean island of Malta with his mother, a small brown snake, a little white dog, and a fat calico cat.

They were very poor, but they loved each other and they lived together in perfect harmony. One day the snake said to Theodore, "You have shown me every kindness in the world. You treat me as if I were just like you. Therefore, I shall now confer upon you the greatest gift a snake can give—magic. Take the ring from around my neck and make a wish."

Theodore did this thing, and at once the kitchen table groaned under the weight of hams, baskets of eggs, strings of garlic, curds of cheese stacked like cordwood, and olives red, black, and green. There were cakes and loaves of dark bread, bottles of wine, and enough olive oil to bathe in.

When Theodore's mother came into their small kitchen, she could not believe her eyes.

"Where did you steal these things?" she asked.

Then Theodore explained how the snake had given him the magic ring from its neck, and how he had made only one wish.

"It's a miracle," the woman gasped. But that night they dined like royalty, and the dog, the cat, and the snake ate right beside them. In the days that followed, Theodore made more wishes. It was not long before their small seaside shanty was a mansion.

The sight of the beautiful new house, which had appeared suddenly, drew the attention of the neighbors. Two crafty fishermen snuck up to the window one night and were greeted by a sight that amazed them.

They saw a spotted cat and a white, frost-faced, bearded dog dining with mother and son. And if this weren't all, they also saw a small brown snake coiled around Theodore's wrist like a bracelet. Moreover, the two observed that when a wineglass was emptied, Theodore merely held out his hand, looked at his gold ring, and said aloud, "I wish for more of the same." Immediately, the glass glittered with ruby-red wine.

"It's that ring," said one of the sly fishermen. "Look how he admires it—the boy's ring is the reason for their riches."

"Indeed," his friend said, "it is a magic ring."

No sooner did he say this than a many-tiered chocolate cake floated out of nowhere and presented itself for the family to eat. That night, when Theodore and his mother were fast asleep and the dog and the cat were dreaming, and only the snake was awake because it wasn't his custom to close his eyes, one of the envious fishermen reached through the window and, grabbing Theodore's ring, pulled it off his finger. Down the road the man ran to the beach where his friend awaited him in a rowboat. Together, the two thieves slipped away into the night.

Now, Theodore, the bearded dog, and the calico cat chased after them—but what could they do without a boat? And without the magic ring to obtain one?

The snake whispered in Theodore's ear, "I have done what I could to make our lives richer, but since you've lost the ring, there's nothing more I can do."

However, the little dog jumped up and cried out, "I am the world's greatest swimmer. I can find the thieves wherever they are."

"Well," said the cat, "I cannot swim, but I have other talents."

"All right," the dog said, "get on my back and away we'll go." And he paddled off into the darkness with the cat perched on his back. Now, after a time, they came to an island. The dog sniffed the sand. "Here's where the thieves have put up for the night," he said, wringing his beard dry with his paws.

The cat disappeared into the bushes, but she quickly returned. "I've found the one with the ring—he's snoring in the hammock, and he keeps the ring in the right side of his mouth."

"Now I know what you mean by 'other talents,'" said the dog. "Can you get the ring back?"

"Certainly," said the calico cat.

"How?"

"I'll use my tail to tickle his throat, and then he'll cough it up fast."

This, indeed, the clever cat accomplished. When the thief spat out the ring, the cat caught it in her paws. Then she and the little white, bearded dog paddled off as before.

Soon, however, the dog sighted land.

"Please let me have a look at the magic ring."

"I wouldn't advise it," said the cat.

"Why not?"

"What if it dropped? Besides, I'm carrying it on my tail, which I have to hold straight up. I don't dare lower it now."

But the bearded dog begged to see the ring, and against her better judgment, the cat lowered her tail.

Ka-plook! The magic ring went right into the sea. And while the two watched in horror, a large spotted mackerel with an enormous jaw spied the ring and swallowed it whole.

Once onshore, the calico cat gave the bearded dog the scolding of his life. "It's all your fault," cried the cat. "Now we've lost the ring forever."

"Not yet. Look, there—"

On the beach was a fisherman, who was reeling in the big-mouthed mackerel that had just swallowed the ring.

"You got the ring back the first time, I'll get it back the second," said the determined little dog.

So, while the fisherman was filleting the fish, the dog put on a show for him. He danced around, doing jigs and reels. He paraded and pirouetted; he wriggled and reeled; he hopped and flopped; and toodled and noodled. And made that fisherman laugh.

"You're quite the circus performer, you are," chuckled the fisherman.

Then he took the insides out of the fish and threw them to the little dog.

"That's for you and the puss," he said.

Now the dog dashed off with the stomach of the mackerel in his mouth, and when he and the cat came to the fine house of Theodore and his mother, he stopped running and squeezed the fish gut, and out came the golden ring.

"You found it!" Theodore exclaimed, but then he did a strange thing. He threw the ring back into the sea.

"Such good luck brings bad luck," he said. "Furthermore, with all the treasure and talent we have in this family, we really don't need any magic."

And they lived happily ever after, but that is not the end of the tale.

For the bearded dog became a circus performer, who danced in the streets of Malta with the organ grinder's monkey. Only this organ grinder didn't have a monkey; instead, he had a cat. And, though the organ grinder looked like a Barbary pirate, he was really a boy named Theodore. And the ring that he wore on his ear, well, you remember the small brown snake, don't you?

AFTERWORD

The name bichon frise means "stirred-up beard" in French, and, as we know, this dog has one. He has a much-traveled history dating back to antiquity; some say as far back as 600–300 B.C. First bred on the island of Malta (like the Maltese and other toy breeds of the Mediterranean), this treasure dog is a terrific swimmer, dancer, and acrobat—not to mention a good luck charm.

Historically, the bichon frise has been a lapdog and a street dog. Once pampered by royalty, he ended up in the seventeenth century as an organ grinder's dancing pet. The dog performed with a monkey, dancing on the street for coins as the organ grinder played favorite melodies.

Our story is a modern Greek folktale, which explains why cats do not trust dogs. The story of the loss of the magic ring is a part of African, Asian, and European pourquoi tales. Sometimes the cat is the hero, sometimes the dog. In our rendition, each animal shares in the heroic quest of finding and returning the magic ring.

The Dog with the Diamond Foot: A Spaniel Tale

ATIS LOVED ARGIA, the most beautiful woman in all of France. Poor Atis was handsome, but he was not rich. So he had little chance with one so fair and highborn as the lovely, the indescribably beautiful Argia. To make matters worse, she had a hard-hearted father, who had forbidden her to marry anyone except a member of the French aristocracy.

The situation was hopeless for the poor lad, except for a certain dog who appeared upon the scene and turned the balance in Atis's favor. They say the dog was made of flesh and bone and thus a mortal dog; but some say she was no more mortal than Cupid.

How it happened was strange enough.

One day a golden spaniel with wistful eyes and a fluffy tail appeared at Atis's door. Heaven-sent, she had the kindest face that ever was, and her manners were finer than her fur. Yet, what a silken coat—why, it shone like sherry in a glass. Moreover, the dog was like no other, for she could speak.

"Sad lad," said she, "how is it that you're not composing a poem for the lovely Argia?"

"How is it that you can talk?" Atis asked.

"I've been sent to help you achieve your love."

"By whom are you sent?"

"I mustn't say. "

Atis lowered his head in despair.

"Don't look down," the deep-eyed spaniel said.

"Why should I not lament my misfortune? Argia will never have me."

"She shall," said the dog.

"And how might that be?"

"I shall appear in your behalf, and, as I am irresistible, she will deny neither of us."

Amused, Atis rubbed the spaniel's glossy fur. She was lovely, of that he was certain. But still, he shook his head.

"A dog can't court a lady," Atis chided.

"I am no mere dog. Squeeze my left foot."

He did as told—and a diamond popped out of the dog's paw.

Atis held the diamond to the light.

"My lucky day has come!" he cried.

"Put your trust in me," the dog said, "and I shall deliver your love to you."

"I trust you with all my heart," Atis said as he admired the diamond.

Now, the pretty spaniel changed Atis into a vagabond minstrel, a ne'er-do-well lad who traveled about the land, singing and dancing for his supper. His sorry-looking clothes were soiled, and his face sooted by many a campfire night. Who would ever guess he was once the handsome youth named Atis?

Off they went, Atis and his performing spaniel. Door to door, they met acclaim, finally arriving at Argia's wrought-iron gate.

Argia appeared above, on the balcony.

"What is this?" she asked. Her red-gold hair flowed over her shoulders, and her eyes twinkled with interest.

"Just a poor lad who wishes to sing you a song."

Argia's attentive eye rested upon the dog.

"Where on earth did you get such a darling spaniel?" she asked.

"My dog is a mere reflection of myself," he quipped.

"Then let us hear your song," she returned with a smile.

Atis opened his mouth, and the most beautiful melody leaped from his lips. He could hardly believe it. But even more astounding was the dog's mellow harmony that accompanied him. She kept up with him—or was it the reverse? Was he keeping up with her? In truth, the enchanting spaniel was doing it all.

Delighted, Argia leaned over the balcony railing.

"I must have your dog—at any price!"

Atis said, "My dog is not for sale, and neither am I."

"Who would want sooty old you?" Argia said, amused.

"You cannot take my spaniel without taking me," returned Atis.

"But I want the dog! And how could a miserable minstrel such as yourself dare to seek the hand of a lady?"

"For love."

Once more Argia regarded the poor singer and the beautiful spaniel. As she gazed into the spaniel's eyes, her heart was suddenly filled with love—not only for one, but for both of them. The spaniel's magic spell was upon Argia, and now she was overcome with love for Atis.

"I don't know what's happening to me," she whispered from above, "but it seems I am now falling head over heels for a woebegone minstrel. Oh, what foolishness!"

She began to wring her hands and pace back and forth.

"Am I not rich enough to win your hand?" Atis asked.

"My father always says, 'Rich of heart is not rich of purse.'"

"Does he now," Atis replied, squeezing his spaniel's paw. Onto the cobbled courtyard the diamonds spilled, ringing musically on the stones.

"I saw that!" cried Argia's father, who was spying on them from the garden. He stared at the dazzling jewels. "The lad can be cleaned up, for heaven's sake, and such a dog is welcome in our house anytime."

And that was how Atis, disguised as a minstrel, wooed and won Argia. Of course, he had the help of a golden-coated, soulful-eyed spaniel, whose portion of magic was no small matter in the affair. Argia's heart was won, however, not by Atis's purse, but by the depth of his love for her. Sometimes it takes a little magic to see love as it really is; and to see those who love as they really are. Eventually, of course, Argia found out who her minstrel boy really was. But, by then, she loved him all the more.

All in all, the riches didn't hurt the match, the marriage, or the treasure chest of Argia's father. For he liked wealthy dogs with bankable paws—and so would you, if you had one.

AFTERWORD

In Europe and in Asia, if you were followed home by a strange dog, it was always a sign of luck, which foretold wealth. Indeed, stray dogs were not considered castaways, but somehow heaven-sent. In Africa and in the Hopi villages of America, it was a bad omen to kick a strange dog. In fact, anyone foolish enough to do such a thing would come down with weakened knees, rheumatism, or some other disease of the leg joints.

How far back in time the belief in dog magic goes, no one can really say. But it is known that prehistoric people would use almost anything belonging to a dog's body, living or dead, as a form of divination. A dog's tail, pointing a certain way, would foretell a migratory route, or the proper time to plant crops. Dog noses and paws have an especially rich lore when it comes to magic. The notion that the squeezing of a dog's paw would produce precious gems is Celtic, but it truly stems from dog worship, a thing that many world cultures have indulged in since the earliest of times. Love of dogs—to the point of believing them to be sacred—also entered the political arena, where dogs became rulers. In ancient Norway, a wolfhound was once elected king because the people reasoned they could be swindled by a man, but not by a dog. In Ethiopia, there was once a dog king who was so honored that his least little growl, or the briefest wag of his tail, would determine the fate of the nation.

The magic spaniel, so-called, was first discussed by the ancient Greek philosopher Pythagoras, who said that the spaniel could capture the last breath of a dying person. By storing away this breath, the spaniel ensured that the person's spirit would live on. Spaniels were thought to be lucky perhaps because of their athleticism as sporting animals. In sixteenth-century Europe, all dogs were considered spaniels, as it was a generic name. The Newfoundland, for example, was thought to be a water spaniel. As "comforte dogs," spaniels took the chill out of drafty castles and chilly carriages, and many a monarch carried one about on the lap or underneath the petticoat. The spaniel's eyes—her most generous feature—are so round, so loving, that people once felt such eyes were psychic, or all-knowing. In any case, it was a great compliment, if you were a woman, to be called "spaniel-eyed."

SOURCES

CHAPTER ONE: THE CREATION DOG: "The Gift of Fire: A Basenji Tale" is adapted from
a story in *God Had a Dog: Folklore of the Dog,* by Maria Leach, Rutgers University Press, 1961.
The narrative style, however, was adapted from an African creation tale told by Spreeboy, a
Rastafarian elder in Castle Gordon, Jamaica, 1996.

CHAPTER TWO: THE TRICKSTER DOG: "Why Dogs Cannot Talk Like People: An Akita
Tale" appears in different form in *The Mythology of Dogs: Canine Legend and Lore Through the
Ages,* by Gerald and Loretta Hausman, St. Martin's Press, 1997. Narrative style inspired by
freelance writer and friend Kenji Okuhira, Los Angeles, California, 1997. • "How Dog
Brought Death into the World: A Husky Tale" was inspired by references in *God Had a Dog:
Folklore of the Dog,* by Maria Leach, Rutgers University Press, 1961; *The Cults of the Dog,* by M.
Oldfield Howey, C. W. Daniel Ltd., 1968; and *The Mythology of Dogs: Canine Legend and Lore
Through the Ages,* by Gerald and Loretta Hausman, St. Martin's Press, 1997. • "First Man and
First Woman's Dog: A Coyote Tale" is retold from a creation tale in *The Gift of the Gila
Monster: Navajo Ceremonial Tales,* introduced and retold by Gerald Hausman, Simon &
Schuster, 1993. Parts of the story were also told to the authors by Navajo artist and poet Jay
DeGroat in 1992.

CHAPTER THREE: THE ENCHANTED DOG: "King Herla's Hound: A Bloodhound Tale"
is retold from *The Mythology of Dogs: Canine Legend and Lore Through the Ages,* by Gerald and
Loretta Hausman, St. Martin's Press, 1997. Narrative style was inspired by *The Ballad Book of John
Jacob Niles,* by John Jacob Niles, Bramhall House, 1961. • "The Ghostly Weaver: A Retriever
Tale" is adapted from an anecdote in *This Doggie Business,* by Edward C. Ash, Hutchinson & Co.,
1934; and from *The Dog Book,* by James Watson, Doubleday, Page & Co., 1916.

CHAPTER FOUR: THE GUARDIAN DOG: "Prince Llewelyn's Gelert: A Wolfhound Tale"
is a retelling from a story in *God Had a Dog: Folklore of the Dog,* by Maria Leach, Rutgers
University Press, 1961; *The Mythology of Dogs: Canine Legend and Lore Through the Ages,* by
Gerald and Loretta Hausman, St. Martin's Press, 1997; and *The Choking Doberman and Other
New Urban Legends,* by Jan Harold Brunvald, W. W. Norton, 1984. Further information was
supplied by a dog owner and visitor to Beddgelert, Wales, who joined the authors on a live
broadcast on Wisconsin Public Radio in 1997. • "The Seven Sleepers: A Saluki Tale" was

inspired by the Christian version of "The Seven Sleepers" in *God Had a Dog: Folklore of the Dog,* by Maria Leach, Rutgers University Press, 1961; the saluki files of the American Kennel Club Library in New York City; and *The Meaning of the Glorious Koran: An Explanatory Translation,* by Marmaduke Pickthall, Alfred A. Knopf, 1992. ❧ "The Thunder Mouth Dog: A Rottweiler Tale" was inspired by a story in the *Larousse Encyclopedia of Mythology,* Prometheus Press, 1959.

CHAPTER FIVE: THE SUPER DOG: "A Dog Named Boye: A Poodle Tale" was inspired by the reproduction of a parliamentary broadsheet, dated 1642, reprinted with notes by Francis Fretwell, the Kennel Club Library in Moore, South Carolina, 1996. ❧ "The Dog Who Married a Princess: A Shar-pei Tale" is a retelling of the story that appears in *God Had a Dog: Folklore of the Dog,* by Maria Leach, Rutgers University Press, 1961; and in *The Mythology of Dogs: Canine Legend and Lore Through the Ages,* by Gerald and Loretta Hausman, St. Martin's Press, 1997.

CHAPTER SIX: THE TREASURE DOG: "The Dog, the Cat, the Snake, and the Ring: A Bichon Frise Tale" is retold from extracts at the American Kennel Club Library in New York City; from the rare book archives of the Richter Library, University of Miami, Miami, Florida; and from *Folktales of All Nations,* by F. H. Lee, Tudor Publishing Co., 1930. The story appears in different form in *The Mythology of Dogs: Canine Legend and Lore Through the Ages,* by Gerald and Loretta Hausman, St. Martin's Press, 1997. ❧ "The Dog with the Diamond Foot: A Spaniel Tale" is retold from the poetry of Jean de la Fontaine in *The Complete Fables of Jean de la Fontaine,* Northwestern University Press, 1988.

The paintings in this book were done in transparent

watercolor on paper handmade especially for Mr. Moser

by Kathryn and Howard Clark at Twinrocker Handmade Papers

in Brookston, Indiana.

•

The text is set in Matthew Carter's Galliard, designed in 1978

based on the sixteenth-century letterforms of Robert Granjon.

The display type is set in Poetica, issued by Adobe Systems in 1996.

Design by Barry Moser